SUPERSTARS OF THE WORLD SERIES

by Brendan Flynn

Cody Koala
An Imprint of Pop!
popbooksonline.com

abdopublishing.com
Published by Pop!, a division of ABDO, PO Box 398166, Minneapolis, Minnesota 55439.

Printed in the United States of America, North Mankato, Minnesota

042018
092018

THIS BOOK CONTAINS RECYCLED MATERIALS

Cover Photo: Robert Beck /Sports Illustrated/Getty Images
Interior Photos: Robert Beck /Sports Illustrated/Getty Images, 1; Shutterstock Images, 5 (top), 5 (bottom right), 6, 17 (bottom left), 17 (bottom right); Steve Lundy/Daily Herald/AP Images, 5 (bottom left); Charlie Riedel/AP Images, 9; Patrick Gorski/Icon Sportswire/AP Images, 11, 21 (bottom); Kyodo/AP Images, 12, 16; David J. Phillip/AP Images, 15, 21 (top); Charles Krupa/AP Images, 17 (top)

Editor: Meg Gaertner
Series Designer: Laura Mitchell

Library of Congress Control Number: 2017963428

Publisher's Cataloging-in-Publication Data
Names: Flynn, Brendan, author.
Title: Superstars of the World Series / by Brendan Flynn.
Description: Minneapolis, Minnesota : Pop!, 2019. | Series: Sports' greatest superstars | Includes online resources and index.
Identifiers: ISBN 9781532160363 (lib.bdg.) | ISBN 9781532161483 (ebook) |
Subjects: LCSH: Baseball players--Juvenile literature. | Sports records--Juvenile literature. | World Series (Baseball)--Juvenile literature.
Classification: DDC 796.35764--dc23

Hello! My name is

Cody Koala

Pop open this book and you'll find QR codes like this one, loaded with information, so you can learn even more!

Scan this code* and others like it while you read, or visit the website below to make this book pop.
popbooksonline.com/superstars-world-series

*Scanning QR codes requires a web-enabled smart device with a QR code reader app and a camera.

Table of Contents

Chapter 1

Springer in the World Series

The World Series happens every fall. Two teams play a series of games against each other. The first team to win four games is the Major League Baseball **champion**.

Watch a video here!

ASTROS
4

George Springer is an **outfielder** for the Houston Astros. Before 2017, the Astros had never won the World Series. Springer helped change that.

The 2017 World Series lasted seven games. Springer hit five **home runs** in the Series! The Astros won 5–1 in Game 7 to become World Series champions.

Chapter 2

Kris Bryant

Kris Bryant plays third base for the Chicago Cubs. The Cubs used to be known as "lovable losers." But Bryant helped them become winners in 2016.

Learn more here!

CUBS

The Cubs needed to win three games in a row to win the World Series. Bryant hit home runs in the first two. He played well in the field, too. The Cubs won!

The Cubs had not won the World Series for more than 100 years.

Chapter 3

Madison Bumgarner

Madison Bumgarner is a **pitcher**. His San Francisco Giants won the World Series in 2010, 2012, and 2014. Bumgarner was a big part of all three championships.

Complete an activity here!

GIANTS

In 2014, he was the winning pitcher in two games. Then he pitched five **shutout** innings to close out Game 7. The Giants were champions again!

Chapter 4

David Ortiz

David Ortiz played for the Boston Red Sox. He hit lots of home runs. He also helped Boston win the World Series three times.

Learn more here!

Ortiz was known as a leader. He showed his teammates how to never give up. The Red Sox came from behind to win many games with help from Ortiz.

Ortiz went by the nickname "Big Papi."

1953

The New York Yankees win their fifth straight World Series. No other team has ever won that many in a row.

2004

David Ortiz helps Boston win the World Series for the first time since 1918.

2014

Madison Bumgarner leads the San Francisco Giants to their eighth World Series win.

2016

Kris Bryant and the Chicago Cubs win the World Series for the first time in more than 100 years.

2017

The Houston Astros win their first World Series with help from outfielder George Springer.

Making Connections

Text-to-Self

Would you ever want to play baseball? Why or why not?

Text-to-Text

Have you read about other great sports players? What makes them great?

Text-to-World

What do you think fans like most about baseball?

Glossary

champion – the best team in a sport.

home runs – hits that go over the outfield fence.

outfielder – a player who guards the areas of the field farthest from the home plate.

pitcher – the player who throws the ball that the batter tries to hit.

shutout – not letting the other team score any runs.

Index

Online Resources

popbooksonline.com

Thanks for reading this Cody Koala book!

Scan this code* and others like it in this book, or visit the website below to make this book pop!

popbooksonline.com/superstars-world-series

*Scanning QR codes requires a web-enabled smart device with a QR code reader app and a camera.